I
Never
Liked
Wednesdays
D0273549

I Never Liked Wednesdays

Roger McGough

With illustrations by
Michael Broad

Barrington Stoke

First published in 2015 in Great Britain by
Barrington Stoke Ltd
18 Walker Street, Edinburgh, EH3 7LP

www.barringtonstoke.co.uk

This story was first published in a different form in
Stowaways (Viking Kestrel, 1986)

Text © 1986 Roger McGough
Illustrations © 2015 Michael Broad

The moral right of Roger McGough and Michael Broad to be identified as the author and illustrator of this work has been asserted in accordance with the Copyright, Designs and Patents Act, 1988

All rights reserved. No part of this publication may be reproduced in whole or in any part in any form without the written permission of the publisher

A CIP catalogue record for this book is available
from the British Library upon request

ISBN: 978-1-78112-462-8

Printed in China by Leo

To Bobby, Lola and Silvan

CONTENTS

Chapter 1
The Call of the Sea

When I was young, I lived in Liverpool and my best friend was a boy called Midge. His real name was Kevin Midgeley, but we called him Midge for short. And he was short, only about three cornflake packets high.

Midge was my best friend and we had lots of things in common. We enjoyed the same things like ... climbing trees, playing footy, going to the pictures and hitting each other really hard. And there were things we didn't enjoy like ... sums, washing behind our ears and eating cabbage.

But there was one big thing that bound Midge and I together, one big thing we had in common. A love of the sea.

The River Mersey is not so busy today. In the old days – but not long, long ago – it was very busy indeed. Those were the days of cargo boats and the big liners that took people across the sea. Large ships sailed out of Liverpool for Canada, America, South Africa, the West Indies, all over the world.

My family had all been to sea. My grandfather and all my uncles, and my great-grandfather too. Six foot six, strong arms rippling in the wind, huge hands grappling with the wheel, soaked in rum and as fierce as a wounded shark – and that was just my granny!

By the time they were 20, most young men in Liverpool had visited parts of the globe I can't even spell.

In my bedroom each night, I used to lie in bed – it's the best place to lie really. I used to lie there, in the winter, and listen to the foghorns sounding all down the river. I could picture ships nosing their way out of the docks into the shipping channel of the River Mersey and out into the Irish Sea. It was exciting. All those far-off places. All those exciting adventures.

Midge and I knew what we wanted to do when we left school – we wanted to become sailors. A captain, an admiral, perhaps one day even a steward. Of course we were only about 10 or 11 at the time, so we thought we'd have a long time to wait.

In fact, the call of the sea came sooner than we'd expected.

Chapter 2
Perfect Child

It was a Wednesday if I remember rightly. I never liked Wednesdays for some reason. I could never spell 'Wednesday' for a start. And it always seemed to rain on Wednesdays. And there were two days to go before the weekend.

Anyway, Midge and I got into trouble at school. I don't remember what for. I suppose it was something silly – perhaps we chewed gum in class, forgot how to read or set fire to the music teacher. I forget now. But the teachers picked on us, nagged us, told us off and did all those boring things that grown-ups get up to sometimes.

And, of course, to make matters worse, my mum and dad were in a right mood when I got home. That was nothing to do with me, of course, because as you have no doubt gathered by now, I was the perfect child. I was clean, polite, well-behaved ... soft in the head. But for some reason my parents clipped me round the ear and sent me to bed early for being childish. Childish! I ask you. I was a child. A child acts his age, and what does he get? A wallop!

So that night in bed, I made up my mind ...

Yes, you've guessed it. In my mind, I could hear the big ships calling out to each other as they slipped out of the Mersey into the oceans beyond. The tugs leading the way like proud little guide dogs.

That's it. We'd run away to sea, Midge and I. I'd tell him the good news in the morning.

Chapter 3
A Lot to Think About

The next two days just couldn't pass fast enough for us.

Midge and I had decided to begin our amazing around-the-world voyage on Saturday morning. That way, if we didn't like it, we would be back in time for school on Monday.

As you can imagine, there was a lot to think about – what clothes to take, how much food and drink. We decided on two jumpers each and wellies in case we ran into storms around Cape Horn.

I'd read somewhere that sailors lived off rum and dry biscuits, so I poured a slug of my dad's Old Navy Rum into an empty pop bottle, topped it up with lemonade, and borrowed a handful of jammie dodgers. I also packed my night vision goggles and Midge settled on a magnifying glass.

On Friday night we met round at Midge's house to make the final plans. He lived with his granny and his sister, so there were no nosy parents to discover what we were up to. We hid all our stuff in the shed in the yard and arranged to meet outside his back door next morning at the crack of dawn, or sunrise – whichever came first.

Chapter 4
The Only People Alive

Sure enough, Saturday morning, when the big hand was on 12 and the little one on 6, Midge and I met with our little bundles under our arms and ran up the street as fast as our tiptoes could carry us.

There was no one about. The streets were silent and deserted except for a few pigeons straddling home after all-night parties. It was a very strange feeling, as if we were the only people alive and the city belonged to us alone. And soon the world would be ours as

well – as soon as we'd stowed away on a ship bound for somewhere far off and exciting.

But by the time we'd got down to the Pier Head where the city meets the River Mersey, a lot more people were up and about. A policeman narrowed his eyes at us.

"Ello, Ello, Ello," he said. "And where are you two going so early in the morning?"

"Fishing," I said.

"Train spotting," said Midge. We looked at each other.

"Just so long as you're not running away to sea," the policeman said.

"Oh no," we trilled. "As if!"

He winked at us. "Off you go then, and remember to look both ways before you cross your eyes."

Chapter 5
Down the Funnel

We left the policeman behind and ran off down onto the landing stage where a lot of ships were tied up.

There was no time to lose – already quite a few of the ships were putting out to sea. Their sirens were blowing and hundreds of seagulls were squeaking in excitement, all tossed into the air like big handfuls of confetti.

Then I spotted a small ship just to the left where the crew were getting ready to cast off. They were so busy with their work that it was easy for Midge and me to slip on board unseen. Up the gang-plank we went and right up onto the top deck where there was no one around.

The sailors were all busy down below, winding in the heavy ropes and revving up the engine that turned the great propellers.

We looked around for somewhere to hide.

"I know, let's climb down the funnel," Midge said.

"Great idea," I said. I was taking the mickey. "Or better still, let's pretend we're a pair of seagulls and perch up there on the mast."

Then I spotted them. The lifeboats.

"Hey, let's climb into one of those," I said. "They'll never look in there – not unless we run into icebergs anyway."

So in we climbed, and no sooner had we covered ourselves with the canvas sheet than there was a great shudder and the whole ship seemed to turn round on itself.

We were off!

Soon we'd be digging for diamonds in the Brazilian jungle or building sandcastles on a tropical island. But we had a while to wait – we knew that. Those places are a long way away. We could be on this ship for days, even months.

So we waited. And waited. And then, after what seemed like hours and hours, we decided to eat our rations. I divided these up equally.

I gave Midge all the rum and lemonade, and I had all the jammie dodgers. When I look back on it now, perhaps it wasn't a good idea, especially for Midge. What with the way the ship was rolling and the fact we'd not had any breakfast, and the excitement, and a couple of swigs of rum from the pop bottle – well, you can guess what happened.

Woooorrppp!

Midge puked. All over the place.

We pulled back the canvas sheet and decided to give ourselves up. We were too far out to sea now for the captain to turn back. The worst he could do was to clap us in irons or shiver our timbers.

We climbed down onto the deck. As Midge staggered to the nearest rail to feed the fishes, I looked out to sea in the hope I'd catch sight of a whale, a shoal of dolphins, or perhaps that I'd see the coast of America coming into view. And what did I see?

The Liver Buildings.

Chapter 6
Stowed Away

Well, anyone can make a mistake, can't they? I mean, we weren't to know we'd stowed away on a ferry.

One that goes from Liverpool across the Mersey to Birkenhead and back again, to and fro all day long.

We'd done four trips hidden in the lifeboat and ended up back in Liverpool. And we'd only been away for about an hour and a half.

"Ah well, so much for running away to sea," we said to each other as we disembarked – although disembowelled might be a better word as far as Midge was concerned.

Rum? Yuck.

We got the bus home. My mum and dad were having their breakfast.

"Aye, aye," my dad said. "Here comes the early bird. And what have you been up to then?"

"I ran away to sea," I said.

"Mm, that's nice," said my mum, as she shook out the cornflakes. "That's nice."

Chapter 7

Fish, Chips and Bubbles

Midge said his granny didn't bat an eyelid when he staggered in all green and peaky. But his sister was a different kettle of fish.

Midge's big sister was called Denise. She was a girl. Not only was she a girl but she was older than Midge by about a hundred years. Her hobbies were dancing, looking at herself in the mirror and bossing little boys around. Midge's biggest regret in life was that he hadn't been born an only child.

Just before the half-term holiday, Midge's gran went to stay with her brother in London for a few days. She left Denise in charge. Midge asked if I could stay and keep him company and everyone agreed. Even Denise, which was a surprise. Perhaps she reckoned that two heads were easier to hit than one.

It was good fun at first because we had the house to ourselves. Denise was out with her friends all day long, having a go at being a teenager. Midge and I had our mates round to play football in the garden or to play cards in the shed. We had fish and chips twice a day and drank Tizer till the bubbles popped out of our ears.

We stayed up late every night, too, because Denise didn't come home until all hours. She was out dancing or playing beauty queens with her daft pals.

Chapter 8
A Sniggerly Lot

The day before Gran was due home, it all changed.

It was a Wednesday. Of course.

We knew something was wrong when Denise got up early and started to tidy up the house. And sing at the same time. If you could call it singing – it was more like the sound of a lorry full of budgies skidding on a wet road. And not only that, but when at last we got out of bed she gave Midge and me a Mars bar each to help her.

In the afternoon, the plot thickened – like the tomato soup we had for lunch. Four of Denise's friends arrived, loaded down with bottles, bread, crisps and dips, sausages, mini pizzas and big hunks of cheese.

“Ooh good, we’re having a party,” Midge said. “How many mates can we invite?”

The girls stopped stabbing sausages and looked at Denise.

It was so quiet you could hear a sausage roll.

“Party? Oh no, we’re not having a party ...” she said. “We’re just ... we’re just ... having a special tea for Jasmin’s birthday. Aren’t we, girls?”

The girls nodded and carried on stabbing sausages.

“Can we come?” I asked.

“No you can’t. It’s girls only,” Denise said.

At this, her friends collapsed into fits of giggles. Sniggerly lot.

"In fact, I thought it might be a good idea if you and Midge stayed at your house tonight," Denise said. "Just for a change."

"But I always stay at my house," I pointed out.

She glared at me. "I mean a change for Midge, you dumb-bell."

"We'd rather stay here," Midge said, "and see the fun."

"Listen you," Denise said, and she brandished a bread knife at her brother. "Let's get one thing straight. I'm having a little tea party this evening for my girl friends and I don't want you here." Then her face went soft, like a cobra with a toy mouse. "Look, here's a twenty," she said. "If you leave now you can both go to the cinema and then go and stay the night at your friend's. See you tomorrow. Bye."

With that, Denise turned back to her smirking pals and they all carried on talking flibberty-gibberish.

Special tea indeed! They were sticking enough sausages onto sticks to feed an army. And Midge and I knew where the army would be coming from. It would be an army of boys from Toll Cross Secondary School.

So without another word, we packed our jammies and toothbrushes into our backpacks, waved a cheery goodbye and set off for the cinema.

As if.

Instead we went to Charlie's Cheeky Chippy for our tea.

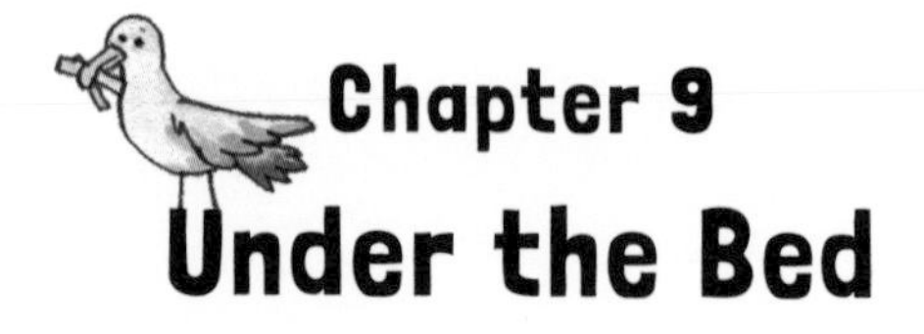

Chapter 9
Under the Bed

After our cheeky chips at Charlie's Chippy, we sneaked back to Midge's. We crept round the back of his house, climbed over the gate and crept up to the shed. We dumped our

backpacks and then we let ourselves in the back door. We tiptoed up the stairs like a couple of deadly secret agents.

As we suspected, the girls were all in the bathroom, wearing out the mirror.

We almost didn't recognise Midge's room when we saw it. It looked like a very messy charity shop. They had rolled up my sleeping bag and put it on top of the wardrobe, and Midge's bed was covered with girls' jackets.

We were wondering whether to turn them all inside-out and tie the arms together, or to chuck them all out of the window, when the dreaded sound of giggles came down the hall towards us.

We did what any highly trained deadly secret agent would have done in the face of danger ... we hid under the bed. Sure enough, in came Denise with two of her crew.

"They'll start to arrive any minute now," Denise said. "Kathleen, you show them up here to leave their coats, and Mel, you see to the drinks when they come down."

The one called Kathleen was a cross between a schoolgirl and a forklift truck.

She moved towards us and plonked herself on the bed. The mattress buckled with pain. Another few centimetres to the left and my face would have been ground into the carpet. As it was, me and Midge were getting very squashed and uncomfortable.

"They're late, aren't they?" Kathleen said.

"Lads always arrive late at parties," Denise told her. "It makes them feel grown-up."

"Midge and Thingy won't try and spoil everything by coming round, will they?" Kathleen asked.

Below the bed, "Thingy" looked at Midge, and Midge looked at "Thingy".

"They'd better not," Denise said, "but just in case they do try to sneak in and spy on us, I'll lock this door."

Again, Midge and I looked at each other and tried not to laugh. Before we could think of an amazing plan of escape the front door bell rang. The girls shrieked, and Kathleen jumped off the bed with a twang of springs. Six feet ran to and fro across the room like clockwork mice, before they disappeared out the door.

Chapter 10
Cartoon Cats

"Come on, this is our chance," Midge said.

I slid out from under the bed with Midge right behind me. But I was only half way across the room when the sound of heavy steps on the stairs warned us that it was too late. There was nothing we could do except wheel around on all fours and squeeze once more back under the bed.

Kathleen led in four pairs of lads' shoes and then disappeared again to answer the door. Three more pairs shuffled in, and then another two. When they were all together, the owners of the shoes acted all weird, not like lads normally do. They either whispered with nerves or talked in too loud voices.

In our heads, Midge and I put pictures to the sounds we could hear. Combs pulling hair into quiffs, hands patting dandruff off jackets, rolling sleeves up and down, pulling up socks, blowing noses.

They were as bad as the girls the way they fussed over their looks. Midge and I almost blushed with shame.

At last, when there was nothing left to squeeze, comb or blow, the lads began to drift out, full of pretend swagger. When the last one had gone, and Midge and I began to wonder if we had a chance of escape after all, the door banged shut.

The sound of the key in the lock put a karate chop to our hopes.

I don't know if the party was a great success or not. I don't know whether they played hide and seek, Scrabble, spin the bottle, pin the tail on the donkey, or 5-a-side football. I don't know who ate most of the sausages on sticks – Forklift Kathleen, I bet. And I don't know who drank most – the same one who left the nasty stain behind the sofa, I suppose. But I do know what music they played. Late into the night, it thudded on the ceiling like an angry neighbour.

But for all the noise and the fact we were lying on a hard floor under a bed piled high with coats, Midge and I fell asleep. That's all we could do, I suppose. Even heroes shake their heads and give up sometimes. It's funny, but we slept like logs, too, and neither of us heard people come into the room to get their jackets and then stomp out again.

The first thing we knew was that it was morning and we were lying under Midge's bed with all our clothes on.

Slowly the horror of our crime loomed over us like the black shadow of the bed.

"What do we do now?" I whispered.

"Sneak downstairs and out," Midge said, "and then we can come back in again as if we'd stayed the night at yours."

We both reckoned that Denise would be fast asleep, but we took no chances. We crept downstairs and out of the back door with as much care as a couple of cartoon cats.

We ran around the houses and then we let ourselves in at the front door, full of the noisy joys of morning. But when we got inside, we were in for a surprise.

There were no signs at all of any party ever happening. The place was as spick and span as Midge's granny could have wished for. Someone must have done all the cleaning the night before, or at the crack of dawn. It was as if we had dreamed the whole thing up.

Chapter 11
A String of Buts

As we ate bowls of cornflakes for breakfast, Midge chatted about how sly and clever big sisters could be. Then the back door slammed open. In marched Denise with our backpacks.

"And what time is this to be coming home?" she demanded.

Midge and I put down our spoons.

"Out all night at your age," Denise said. "It's disgusting."

"We haven't been anywhere ..." we protested feebly. "We stayed at ..."

But before the fibs could get in order, Denise's eyes looked into mine.

"Guess who I just bumped into in the street?" she said. "Your mother. And she asked if you were enjoying your stay here, and behaving yourself, and why not bring Midge home at the weekend?"

In my mouth, the milk turned sour.

"I know what happened last night," Denise went on. "You can't fool me. You both tried to run away to sea again, didn't you?"

"No we didn't ..." I said.

"No ..." said Midge. "We ... er ... no ... er ... er ..."

We began to realise that the truth might sound even worse.

"Just wait till Gran hears about this," Denise snapped. She turned back to me. "I bet your father will give you such a clip round the ear."

"But ..."

"But ..."

"But ... but ..."

"But ... but ... but ..."

Midge and I stammered out a string of buts, but Denise butted in again.

"Unless of course," she said, "we can come to some arrangement."

And so, of course, we came to some arrangement.

We never mentioned the party to Midge's granny – or to anybody else for that matter – and Denise said nothing about our running away to sea again.

I know we didn't run away, but it seemed easier to let Denise think that we had. Or did she? Maybe she even knew the truth all along. Maybe she locked the bedroom door on purpose, because she knew that we were hiding under the bed.

You can never tell with big sisters.

Maybe that's why I never liked Wednesdays. It's best to be a stowaway or a secret agent on another day. Take it from me, it just won't work on a Wednesday.